LUCY LANCASTER
Is Totally in Control

By **Willow Coven**
Illustrated by **Priscilla Burris**

LITTLE SIMON
New York   Amsterdam/Antwerp   London
Toronto   Sydney/Melbourne   New Delhi

This book is a work of fiction. Any references to historical events, real people, or real places are used fictitiously. Other names, characters, places, and events are products of the author's imagination, and any resemblance to actual events or places or persons, living or dead, is entirely coincidental.

LITTLE SIMON
An imprint of Simon & Schuster Children's Publishing Division
1230 Avenue of the Americas, New York, New York 10020
First Little Simon hardcover edition May 2025
© 2025 by Simon & Schuster, LLC
Also available in a Little Simon paperback edition.
All rights reserved, including the right of reproduction in whole or in part in any form.
LITTLE SIMON is a registered trademark of Simon & Schuster, LLC, and associated colophon is a trademark of Simon & Schuster, LLC.
LUCY LANCASTER is a trademark of Simon & Schuster, LLC.
For information about special discounts for bulk purchases, please contact Simon & Schuster Special Sales at 1-866-506-1949 or business@simonandschuster.com.
The Simon & Schuster Speakers Bureau can bring authors to your live event. For more information or to book an event contact the Simon & Schuster Speakers Bureau at 1-866-248-3049 or visit our website at www.simonspeakers.com.
Book design by Chrisila Maida
Manufactured in the United States of America 0325 LAK
10 9 8 7 6 5 4 3 2 1
CIP data for this book is available from the Library of Congress.
ISBN 9781665964036 (hc)
ISBN 9781665964029 (pbk)
ISBN 9781665964043 (ebook)

Contents

Chapter 1	SKYE SIMMONS-YOUNG	1
Chapter 2	FLOWER POWER	13
Chapter 3	ALL FUN AND BOARD GAMES	27
Chapter 4	COUSINS 4EVER	39
Chapter 5	SEARCHING FOR THE CURE	49
Chapter 6	BORIS THE GUARD DOG	59
Chapter 7	NO MORE MAGIC!	71
Chapter 8	RUNAWAY HICCUPS	81
Chapter 9	RISE, STUFFED ANIMALS, RISE	93
Chapter 10	WANDS AND WISHES	109

Chapter 1

SKYE SIMMONS-YOUNG

Lucy woke up with the birds outside. *Tweet, tweet, tweet!*

On the weekends Lucy liked to stay in bed a little longer, but this was no ordinary weekend.

Today she was going to see her favorite cousin, Skye Simmons-Young!

When Lucy and Skye were little, they saw each other all the time. They played hopscotch in Lucy's driveway, rode their bikes at the park, and even went trick-or-treating together.

But a few years ago, Skye's family moved far away. Now Lucy only got to see them once in a while instead of every day.

That's why she was over the moon that Skye, Aunt Jackie, and Aunt Erika were coming for a visit this weekend!

Lucy slipped on her glasses, stepped into her slippers, and threw open the curtains.

Her body tingled with excitement, like there was magic in the air. And Lucy knew a thing or two about magic!

Lucy went over her plans for the day. First she and Skye would play a board game called Snails and Letters. Then she and Skye would make charm bracelets together.

Lucy put on a dress with fringes at the hem. Whenever she moved, the fringes swayed back and forth. She couldn't wait to show it off to Skye!

Breakfast was toast, milk, and orange slices. Mmm, oranges! Lucy pushed them to the side and munched on the toast first. She wanted to save the best for last.

Lucy's mom walked into the kitchen holding her phone.

"Your Aunt Jackie just called," she said. "They're going to eat lunch on the road and arrive here around one thirty."

One thirty? Lucy looked at the clock on the wall. There were still HOURS until one thirty!

Hoping to make time move faster, Lucy raced through her breakfast. She wolfed down her toast and chugged her milk.

But sadly, that's not how time works. The clock kept ticking at the same speed. The same SLOW speed.

As Lucy grabbed one of the orange slices on her plate, she hiccupped.

SQUELCH!

The orange slice exploded in Lucy's hands, spraying juice and pulp everywhere. Under the table, her toes tingled.

"Was that a hiccup?" Lucy's mom said. "That's what happens when you gobble down your breakfast so fast."

Lucy wiped the orange pulp off her glasses. She knew her hiccups had nothing to do with her breakfast.

They had EVERYTHING to do with magic!

Chapter 2

FLOWER POWER

Lucy looked down at her dress and sighed loudly. There were orange spots all over it!

She tried to wipe them off, but it was no use. She would have to change clothes.

And it was all her magic's fault.

A lot of kids wished they were magic. But Lucy wasn't one of them. Because her magic seemed to have a mind of its own. It just hiccupped out of her at the worst possible times.

Lucy's magic was always a surprise!

Back in her room, Lucy changed into jeans and a T-shirt with a flower printed on it.

It wasn't as exciting as her dress with the fringes, but it was nice and comfy to play in.

Lucy looked at herself in the mirror and put her hands on her hips.

"No more hiccups!" she said to her own reflection. "Not today!"

Lucy wanted her weekend with Skye to be perfect, and she didn't want to let magic get in the way of her plans!

Lucy's mom stepped into her room and looked around.

"You have to tidy this place up before Skye gets here," she said. "And hurry. They'll be here soon."

Lucy was so excited to see Skye, she didn't even mind having to clean up. She started putting everything away in her closet.

Lucy had just finished lining up her stuffed animals when she heard the sound of car doors outside.

"Skye's here!" she yelled, dashing to the front door as fast as she could.

"Skye!" Lucy screamed.

"Lucy!" Skye screamed.

The girls hugged each other tightly. Then they performed their secret handshake: left hand high five, right hand high five, three claps, left elbow bump, right elbow bump, three twirls, left foot low five, right foot low five, and then POSE!

Aunt Jackie chuckled.

"This handshake gets more complicated every time," she said, shaking her head.

"Hi, Aunt Jackie! Hi, Aunt Erika!" Lucy said, throwing her arms around both aunts.

Then Skye gasped and pointed at Lucy's shirt.

"A flower!" Skye pointed to the big flower clip in her hair. "We're matching!"

Lucy smiled. Maybe it WAS a good thing that the orange had sprayed her dress.

"A bunny gave this flower to me," Skye told Lucy, tapping her flower clip. "She left it on my windowsill."

"Really?" Lucy asked.

Skye loved making up stories. Sometimes it was hard to know what was a Skye story and what was a Skye truth.

Do bunnies REALLY bring flowers to your window in Skye's new neighborhood? Lucy wondered.

Either way, it didn't matter. The two cousins went to Lucy's room.

"I planned out the perfect day," Lucy said. "Have you ever played the game Snails and Letters?"

Skye shook her head. "No, never."

"Don't worry. I'll teach you!" Lucy said, clapping her hands. She loved teaching people new games!

HICCUP!

The hiccup escaped Lucy's mouth before she could stop it.

A second later, a clatter came from inside her closet.

When Lucy pulled the door open, an avalanche of games, dress-up clothes, and stuffed animals came pouring out.

"GAH!" she shrieked.

Chapter 3

ALL FUN AND BOARD GAMES

"Sorry for the mess," Lucy stammered. But Skye just giggled.

"I know what you did," she said, nudging Lucy in the ribs. "You shoved everything in your closet right before I came, right?"

"Nooo!" Lucy protested.

But Lucy couldn't say hiccups had caused the mess.

The two girls began putting all the stuff back.

"Hey, what's this?" Skye asked, holding up a box with the words THE TWISTED TOWER printed on it.

"I won that game at the spelling bee," Lucy explained. "I haven't played it yet, though."

"Then let's play it now!" Skye said.

Lucy would have rather played Snails and Letters, but that game was still buried somewhere under all her stuff. Besides, Skye was already opening the box.

Lucy began reading the instruction booklet aloud.

"'You are a wizard-in-training,'" Lucy read. "'You must climb to the top of the tower and receive the grand wizard's blessing—'"

Without waiting for Lucy to finish, Skye drew the first card.

"We'll figure it out as we play," she said.

To climb up the tower, Lucy and Skye had to do whatever the cards told them to do. They spun around in circles, hopped twenty times on one foot, and recited silly tongue twisters.

Finally they had only one card left to make it to the top of the tower and win the game.

Skye stood up to read the last card.

"'Your mission is to roll a six on the die,'" she said in her deepest, most serious voice. "'And you only have three tries.'"

"We can do this!" Lucy said, feeling her heart start to beat faster.

Skye rolled first. She got a two. Not even close!

Then it was Lucy's turn to roll. She got a five.

"We only have one more chance," Lucy said.

Skye cupped both hands around the die and shook it with all her might.

"Please, please be a six!"

Lucy let out a hiccup. A LOUD hiccup.

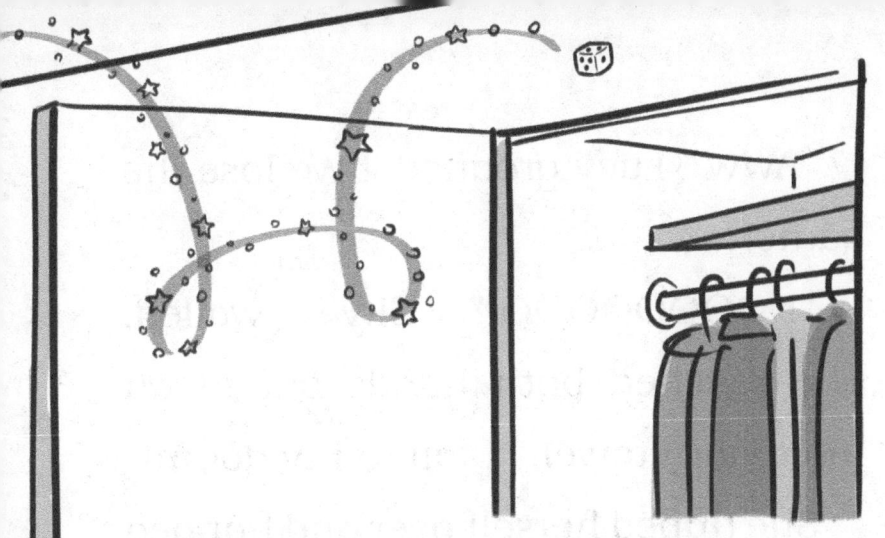

The die flew out of Skye's hand . . . and into the air! It sailed all around the room, bouncing off the walls and the ceiling.

"Whoa!" Skye exclaimed, ducking out of the way. Finally the die landed on the board.

Her toes still tingling, Lucy peered at the die. It was a one.

"Aww," Lucy groaned. "We lose the game!"

"NOOOOOOOO!" Skye wailed. She reached both hands out to an imaginary tower. "I fall to my doom!"

She tipped herself over and flopped onto the bed.

Lucy giggled and tipped herself onto the bed too.

They kept tipping themselves over and over until they laughed so hard, their stomachs hurt.

Once they caught their breaths, Skye said, "Did you see how that die flew around the room? That was like magic, don't you think?"

"Magic?" Lucy asked, laughing nervously. "I don't think so!"

Chapter 4

COUSINS 4EVER

After a few more rounds of The Twisted Tower, the cousins were ready to play something else.

The new board game had turned out to be fun, but now Lucy wanted to get back on plan.

It was time for charm bracelets!

Lucy poured out all the beads from the bracelet kit. The girls began to sort them. There were so many shapes, colors, and patterns!

Skye started her bracelet with a simple pattern. Two round beads, one butterfly, three square beads, one butterfly.

Lucy didn't know where to start. What kind of bracelet should she make?

Then, looking at all the beads laid out in front of her, she was struck with a great idea.

"Don't look this way until I'm finished, okay?" Lucy said.

The girls turned so they sat back-to-back. Lucy quickly started gathering beads and stringing them together.

Yes! Lucy had just enough beads to spell "COUSINS."

Skye kept working on her own bracelet, but her curiosity was too strong.

"Can I look yet?" she asked, peeking over her shoulder.

"Not yet!" Lucy replied.

She strung adorable heart charms on each end of the bracelet.

NOW she was ready.

Lucy turned around. "Okay, you can look at my—"

Before she could finish her sentence, she felt another hiccup bubbling up inside her. Oh no!

Lucy sucked in a mouthful of air, puffed out her cheeks, and held her breath. No hiccups could escape her now!

Skye turned around.

"Ooh!" she squealed. "Are we playing Don't Laugh? First one to laugh loses!"

Lucy didn't know that game, but as long as she could keep the hiccup inside, she was okay.

Skye stood up and started dancing. Then she pushed her nose up like a pig and started to snort.

Lucy couldn't hold it in any longer. She let out a giant laugh-i-cup, which is when you laugh and hiccup at the same time. It sounded like this:

WHOOFICUPOOF!

Skye burst out laughing too.

"Wow, you win, Lucy," she said. "That was the funniest sound I've ever heard!"

But then Lucy looked down at her bracelet and gasped. All the beads that had spelled out "COUSINS" had turned into regular old beads.

"Cute," Skye said, looking at Lucy's bracelet.

But Lucy didn't think it was so cute. In fact, she had had enough. She couldn't keep letting her hiccups get in the way.

"That's it," decided Lucy, standing up. "We have to get rid of these hiccups once and for all!"

Chapter 5

SEARCHING FOR THE CURE

Lucy knew her hiccups weren't any ordinary ones.

But could getting rid of magical hiccups be THAT different from getting rid of regular hiccups?

She wasn't sure, but she was willing to try!

Lucy and Skye went to the kitchen and filled a plastic cup with water.

"My friend Bruce Bickerson says that drinking water cures hiccups," Lucy explained. Then she took two big gulps of water.

"Wait," Skye said, shaking her head. "You can't just drink water the regular way. You have to drink from the other side of the cup!"

"The other side? How?" Lucy imagined herself drinking from those hamster water bottles, where the water came out from the bottom.

"I'll show you," Skye said. She filled her own cup so they could do it together.

"You have to bend over like this, and then put your mouth on the far side of the cup."

Skye draped herself over the seat of the chair, kind of like a towel hanging over a rack. Then she put her lips on the far side of the cup's rim.

Lucy followed Skye's twisty pose, but it was a lot harder than it looked. Lucy tilted the glass a little too far, a little too fast, and the water splashed all over her face.

That made Skye laugh, and she accidentally splashed water on herself too. They were both soaked!

As they wiped themselves off, Skye noticed a pitcher of iced tea. It was sitting out on the counter for the grown-ups, along with some lemon wedges.

"I watched a video once where someone drank lemon juice to stop their hiccups," Skye said. "Want to try it?"

"I'll only try it if you do too," Lucy replied.

"Let's do it!" Skye said.

Lucy picked up a lemon wedge and handed another one to Skye. The girls counted to three, then bit into their lemons.

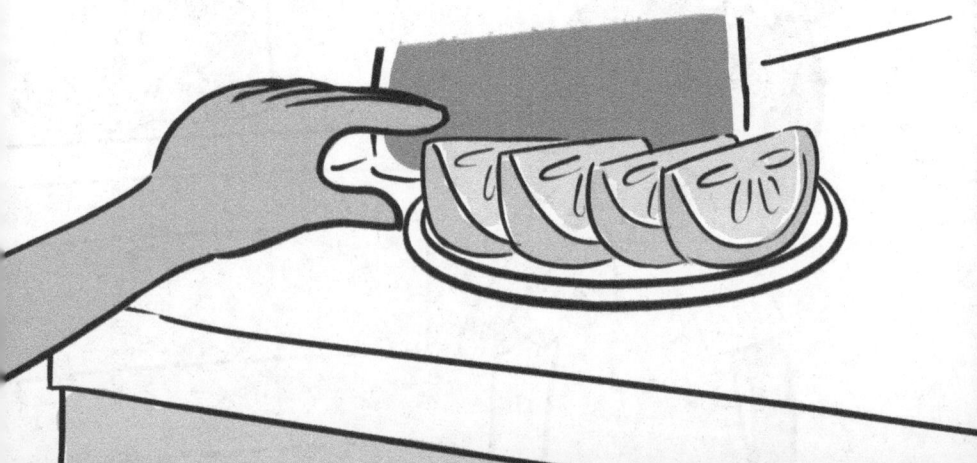

"Ew! So sour!" Lucy shouted, squeezing her eyes shut.

Skye puckered up her face too. But she said, "Yum! So sour!"

"I can't believe you LIKE this!" Lucy said, shuddering from all the sourness in her mouth.

Meanwhile, Skye popped the whole lemon wedge into her mouth. Then she gave Lucy a big, evil lemon-peel smile.

"Arrrgh!" Lucy squealed. "It's a lemon monster!"

She ran out of the kitchen at top speed. Skye followed right behind her.

Chapter 6

BORIS THE GUARD DOG

Lucy and Skye ran into the living room, where the grown-ups were sitting and drinking iced tea.

"What are you girls up to?" Aunt Erika asked.

"Trying to get rid of my hiccups," Lucy replied.

"When I was your age, my sister used to scare the hiccups right out of me!" Aunt Jackie said, nudging Lucy's mom in the ribs.

"That's what I was trying to do too!" Skye said.

Lucy's mom chuckled. "Then maybe Lucy needs an even bigger scare," she suggested.

A BIGGER scare? "Uh, no, thank you," Lucy mumbled.

Skye didn't hear her, though, because she had already dashed out of the living room.

Lucy followed her. But when she reached her own room, the door slammed shut from the inside.

A few seconds later, the door opened just a tad, and Skye plopped Lucy's stuffed dog on the ground in front of it.

"This is Boris, the guard dog," she said from behind the door. "He is guarding the door so you can't come in until my surprise is ready. No peeking, or else this guard dog will lick your face one hundred times!"

Kicked out of her own room! Lucy couldn't believe it. Then . . .

HICCUP!

Oh no, Lucy thought. What was going to happen now?

She didn't have to wait to find out.

SWISH SWOOSH. Boris, the stuffed guard dog, started to move!

He sat up straight and faced Lucy with a very serious look on his puppy-dog face.

"I am the guardian of this room," the dog said. "None shall pass."

YIKES! Her magic had brought Boris to life!

"Shhh, Boris," Lucy whispered urgently. "You have to hide, or else someone will see you!"

But Boris sniffed knowingly.

"I can smell a trap from a mile away," he said. "You're trying to get me to leave my post!"

Ugh. This was one smart stuffed guard dog! Lucy thought.

It was time to use the art of misdirection.

"Look!" she said, pointing down the hallway. "A squirrel!"

"Squirrel?!" Boris's ears perked up. He dashed down the hallway in the blink of an eye.

Lucy followed, right on his tail. But just as she reached out to grab him, Boris took off into the air!

"Come down from there!" Lucy ordered, jumping up to catch him. She jumped as high as she could, but Boris still hovered just out of reach.

From above Lucy's head, Boris barked out a warning.

"Lucyyyy," Skye called from the other side of the door. "Are you being mean to Boris out there?"

"No!" Lucy called back, trying not to panic. Skye could open the door at any moment and discover Boris floating in the air!

Lucy jumped as high as she possibly could. Her hand barely grazed Boris's tail before she fell, landing with a THUMP!

"Ow!" she said. But what surprised her more was that she was now sitting on something that hadn't been on the floor moments before.

It was her magic spell book!

Chapter 7

NO MORE MAGIC!

Perfect timing!

Lucy flipped open the book, looking for a spell to turn Boris back into a regular, nonfloating, nonmagical stuffed dog.

But what the *Book of Spells* offered her was even better.

The No More Hiccups Spell

Are you stuck with a case of the hiccups that won't go away? Are they interrupting all your plans for the day? If you want to stop your hiccups for good, this is the spell for you!

Take a deep breath and count backward from ten to one. Then chant the following spell—one line at a time, from right to left.

"Are you sure this is a good idea?" Boris asked, peeking over her shoulder.

But Lucy ignored him. She rubbed her hands together happily. This spell would solve ALL her problems, and then she could get back to playing with Skye!

Lucy followed the directions and read the spell aloud, line by line.

A swirl of magic rose from Boris. As he fell to the floor, the magic swirl lifted the *Book of Spells* into the air.

Then the book flew right through Lucy's closed bedroom door . . . which was exactly where Skye was!

Lucy picked up the lifeless stuffed dog and held her breath for a second. How could she explain her *Book of Spells* to Skye?

"Boris, you can go off duty now!" Skye declared from inside the room. It was as if she hadn't noticed the book at all.

Lucy opened the door. Skye wore Lucy's long cape from her dress-up box, and there was a pointy hat on her head.

"Behold! I am Skye Simmons-Young, the evil witch of Brewster!" she shouted. "I am here to scare the hiccups out of you!"

But Lucy was too distracted to be scared. She peered around the room, looking for any sign of her *Book of Spells*. Thankfully, it was nowhere to be seen.

That made her so happy, she did a little dance. Then she hugged Skye.

"It's okay!" she told her cousin. "My hiccups are gone now!"

"Oh," Skye said, sounding a little disappointed. "So I don't have to scare you anymore?"

"Nope!" Lucy replied.

"Well, let's play something else," Skye said, pulling off the wizard's hat.

And that's when it happened.

Skye HICCUPPED!

Chapter 8

RUNAWAY HICCUPS

Lucy looked at Skye.

Skye looked at Lucy.

HICCUP!

"I think I'm the first person in the world to CATCH hiccups from someone!" Skye exclaimed.

Lucy was speechless.

Lucy couldn't believe her eyes.

From the closet behind Skye, all the stuffed animals were rising into the air!

For the first time ever, she hoped a hiccup would come out of her and stop the stuffed animals. But of course, she had just magicked her magical hiccups away.

Skye had no idea what was happening behind her. She let out another hiccup, and magic crackled through the air.

Lucy could feel Boris trying to lift out of her arms. She squeezed him with all her might to keep him still.

"Is Boris's tail wagging?" Skye gasped.

Lucy couldn't fight the magic any longer. ZOOM! Boris rocketed out of Lucy's arms and joined all the other stuffed animals near the ceiling.

Skye screamed with delight.

"Wow! Are these stuffed animals MAGIC?" Skye said.

Lucy pretended not to hear the question. Instead, she jumped up, trying to catch the stuffed animals and pull them down. But they floated just out of reach.

When Skye reached out HER arms, though, all the stuffed animals floated down right toward her. They snuggled against her cheek, gave her little hugs, and patted her on the head.

"Wait a second," Skye said, looking at Lucy. "Maybe the magical one is ME?"

"Uh, no!" Lucy said quickly. "These are actually, um . . . stuffed robots! My friend Bruce invented them. They can read your mind!"

"Whoa, that's the coolest thing—" **HICCUP!**

Another hiccup escaped from Skye. The stuffed animals drifted to the floor and started cleaning up the messy room.

"Wow!" Skye clapped her hands with glee. "I need to show this to my moms."

"No!" cried Lucy. "It's a secret! I mean—that's what Bruce said."

"Secret, smeecret," Skye said. "The world needs to see how cool this is."

She ran out of the room to get her moms, leaving Lucy surrounded by magic stuffed animals.

How was she going to get out of this mess?

Chapter 9

RISE, STUFFED ANIMALS, RISE

"Gah!" Lucy cried, pacing around in circles. "What do I do?"

She had magicked away her hiccups, but now she felt even more out of control than ever.

That was when Boris floated over to her, carrying the *Book of Spells*.

Just in time! Lucy had to reverse her last spell. And fast!

Lucy grabbed the book and flipped it open.

How to Catch the Hiccups

(For witches in a big rush)

Take a short breath and count backward from five to one. Then chant the following spell—one line at a time, from right to left.

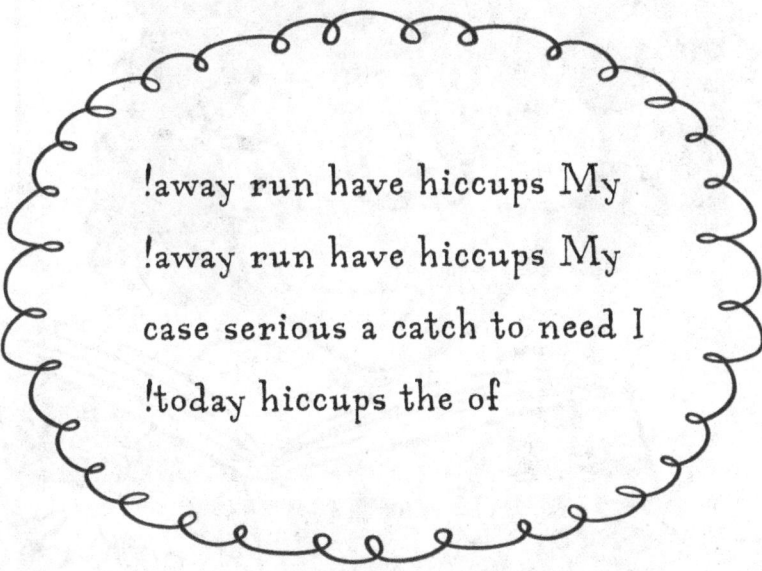

!away run have hiccups My
!away run have hiccups My
case serious a catch to need I
!today hiccups the of

Lucy couldn't have chanted the spell any faster. As she read the last line aloud, she heard Skye practically dragging her moms down the hallway.

"Oh, honeybun, what's the rush?" Aunt Jackie asked.

"You'll see," Skye replied. Then she cleared her throat. "I now present to you . . . FLYING STUFFED ANIMALS!"

Skye and her moms appeared in the doorway. Lucy was still standing in the middle of the room. But now, all the stuffed animals lay quietly on the floor.

"Rise, stuffed animals, rise!" Skye declared, throwing up her arms.

But nothing happened.

"Why isn't it working?" she said, looking completely puzzled.

Lucy couldn't help feeling bad for Skye. She picked up Boris, tossed him into the air, and caught him in her arms.

"Ta-da!" Lucy exclaimed. "Flying stuffed animals!"

The aunts shook their head and chuckled.

"Glad you girls are having fun," Aunt Erika said. Then they both turned away to leave.

"What happened?" Skye asked, slumping onto the bed. "Why didn't the robots work?"

Lucy sat down on the bed too.

"Bruce is still working on them," she said. "They're not perfect yet."

"But I wanted to see them again!" Skye sulked.

"I know," Lucy said. "But, hey, why don't we play something else? Your choice!"

That made Skye perk up.

"I really liked being magic," she said. "Let's keep playing that in the backyard!"

Skye filled her arms with stuffed animals and raced outside. Lucy carried the rest. They were piled so high in her arms, she could barely see where she was walking!

As Lucy headed toward the door to the backyard, Boris slid off the pile and landed on the floor.

Lucy groaned. There was no way to pick him up without dropping all the other stuffed animals from her arms.

And right on cue . . .

HICCUP!

Lucy's toes tingled. A little swirl of magic lifted Boris up off the floor and placed him back onto the pile.

Lucy smiled. She was grateful to have her hiccups—and her magic—back!

Chapter 10

WANDS AND WISHES

In the backyard, Lucy and Skye lined up the stuffed animals on the edge of the grass. Then they each found a stick to use as their wand.

"Witches NEVER let their wands out of their hands," Skye said with a serious face.

Secretly, Lucy knew witches didn't need wands to cast spells. But she didn't say that to Skye.

The girls waved around their wands, casting spells on the clouds in the sky, on the ants on the ground, and on the stuffed animals.

It turned out, playing make-believe witches was fun. Even when you were a real witch!

Before they knew it, Lucy and Skye were called for dinner. The weather was nice, so they all decided to eat outside in the backyard.

After helping to set the table outside, Skye and Lucy sat down.

"Sorry, girls, but no sticks at the table," Aunt Erika said.

"They're wands," Skye corrected.

"Boris can watch over our wands while we eat," Lucy suggested. "We can trust him to take good care of them."

"Hmm," Skye said. "You're right. We can make a special exception."

They placed their wands on the grass next to Boris. Now they could go back to eating!

Aunt Erika had brought her famous curry for dinner. It was just the right amount of spicy, and a little bit sweet. It was so tasty, Lucy had seconds!

After dinner, the two girls changed into their pajamas. They watched Skye's favorite cartoon, *Emerald Enchanter Serena*.

After laying out their sleeping bags, Skye carefully placed their wands near their pillows.

"You never know when you'll need to use magic," she said.

Lucy couldn't agree more with that!

Then the two girls snuggled into their sleeping bags and turned off the lights.

"I wish we could have sleepovers like this every night," Lucy said.

"Me too," Skye agreed. Then she looked at Lucy. "You know what I also wish? I wish magic was actually real!"

"Yeah," Lucy said slowly. "I bet magic is really fun."

The truth was magic was fun sometimes. Today had been a great day, even with all the hiccups. No, maybe BECAUSE of the hiccups.

Lucy had to admit, she was glad she hadn't magicked away her hiccups forever and ever.

"Maybe we'll dream about flying through the sky on our broomsticks," Lucy said just before drifting off to sleep.

And that's exactly what they did.

Check out the next book starring

LUCY LANCASTER

STRUM, STRUM, TWANG, TWANG.

Lucy loved making the guitar sing!

Her guitar teacher, Mr. Martin, clapped his hands.

"Great job, Lucy!" he said. "You're getting better and better every week."

Lucy beamed with pride.

An excerpt from *Lucy Lancaster in the Spotlight*

Back when she first started guitar lessons at the Brewster Community Center, she couldn't even keep the guitar from sliding off her lap. And pressing on the strings hurt her fingers.

Now, here she was, playing full songs!

"Listen up, everyone," Mr. Martin said. "We're going on a short field trip!"

A field trip? They'd never had a field trip at the end of class before!

Lucy and her two classmates, Karina Kam and Gabe Gomez, lined

An excerpt from *Lucy Lancaster in the Spotlight*

up by the door as quickly as they could.

Mr. Martin led them down the hallway to another room.

When he flicked on the lights, Lucy saw they were in a big room with a stage. It was smaller than the gymnasium at Lucy's school, but much fancier.

Mr. Martin bounded up the steps and stood under the spotlight on the stage.

"Strum roll, please!" he called.

An excerpt from *Lucy Lancaster in the Spotlight*